Table of Contents

Frog and the Green Dragon

Frog and Friends
Frog Saves the Day

Written by Eve Bunting
Illustrated by Josée Masse

To Shane, my favorite grandson

—*Eve*

For my lovely aunt Céline

—*Josée*

This book has a reading comprehension level of 2.0 under the ATOS® readability formula.
For information about ATOS please visit www.renlearn.com.
ATOS is a registered trademark of Renaissance Learning, Inc.

Lexile®, Lexile® Framework and the Lexile® logo are trademarks of MetaMetrics, Inc.,
and are registered in the United States and abroad. The trademarks and names of other
companies and products mentioned herein are the property of their respective owners.
Copyright © 2010 MetaMetrics, Inc. All rights reserved.

Sleeping Bear Press™

315 E. Eisenhower Parkway, Ste. 200
Ann Arbor, MI 48108
www.sleepingbearpress.com

Printed and bound in the United States.

10 9 8 7 6 5 4 3 2 1 (case)
10 9 8 7 6 5 4 3 2 1 (pbk)

Library of Congress Cataloging-in-Publication Data • Bunting, Eve, 1928- • Frog and friends : Frog
saves the day / written by Eve Bunting; • illustrated by Josée Masse. • pages cm • Summary: "A
beginning reader book containing two stories featuring Frog and his friends, where the friends
mistake a train for a terrible dragon and Frog rescues a baby possum after it falls into a river"—
Provided by publisher. • ISBN 978-1-58536-809-9 (hard cover) — ISBN 978-1-58536-810-5 (paper
back) • [1. Frogs—Fiction. 2. Animals—Fiction. 3. Friendship—Fiction.] I. Masse, Josée, illustrator. II.
Title. III. Title: Frog saves the day. • PZ7.B91527Fse 2013 • [E—dc23 • 2013004091

One night Raccoon came to Frog.

"I do not sleep well," she told him.

"Every night a big, big, big noise wakens me."

"That is terrible," Frog said. "What is it?"

"I do not know," Raccoon said. "I hide under the tree leaves. I put my paws over my ears. Whatever it is, it comes every night. It has a roar like thunder. But it isn't thunder."

"Oh my!" Frog croaked. "Is it close to us?"

"No. It is far away," Raccoon whispered.

"But I am afraid it will come closer. I think it is something bad."

"Oh my!" Frog said again. He closed his eyes, thinking.

At last he said, "You and I and our friends will go together and find out what it is. It is better to face up to what frightens you."

That night they set out, Frog, Raccoon, Possum, Squirrel, Chameleon, Rabbit, and little Jumping Mouse.

"I do not hear any roar like thunder," Possum said.

"You will," Raccoon told her. "It will

make your fur stand on end."

They walked farther.

"Ooo! I hear it," little Jumping Mouse said.

Raaaaaaaaaaa-cla cla cla!

They hid themselves in the long grass.

Raccoon held Frog's hand. "I am so scared," she whispered.

The thunder roar was louder.

Raaaaaaaaaaaa-cla cla cla!

"My fur is standing on end," Possum

moaned.

The big bad thing came around a bend.

It had one giant shining eye.

It had no legs.

It had a long, stringy body.

"Like a snake. Only bigger," Chameleon whispered. "Much, much bigger."

"Look! It leaves a silver track," Rabbit whispered. "Like a snail track, only bigger. **Much, much bigger.**"

"I am sorry to tell you," Frog said. "I

think it is a big green dragon."

Possum screamed, **"Oh no!** I can see

inside it."

"Look at all the people it has eaten,"

Squirrel squeaked. "I can see them."

They were shocked!

Rabbit shuddered. "That is gross!"

"I am glad no one can see inside me," Chameleon said. "Today I ate pillbugs, beetles, white worms, and roaches. Inside of me would not be pretty!"

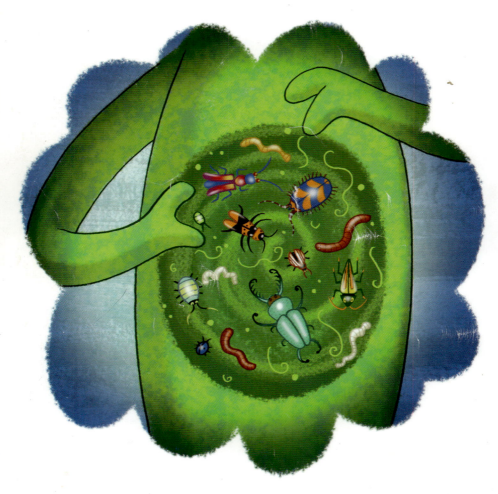

"I am glad Mrs. Brown cannot see inside me," Squirrel said. "Today I dug up all her tulip bulbs. And ate them."

Little Jumping Mouse gasped, "Mrs. Brown will be very angry!"

"What can we do, Frog?" Rabbit asked.

"This is a terrible dragon."

Frog fanned himself with an oak leaf.

"I am glad we came and saw," he said.

"Now we know. This dragon only eats people.

He is not looking for us. We are safe."

Raccoon closed her eyes. "Thank goodness," she whispered.

They high-fived each other.

"Oh, but it is sad for people," little Jumping Mouse said. "How can we help them, Frog?"

"We will sing a sad song for them," Frog said. "That is all we can do."

They joined paws and claws and hands and sang a very sad song.

It was so sad that they all cried.

Then they felt better and went back

home.

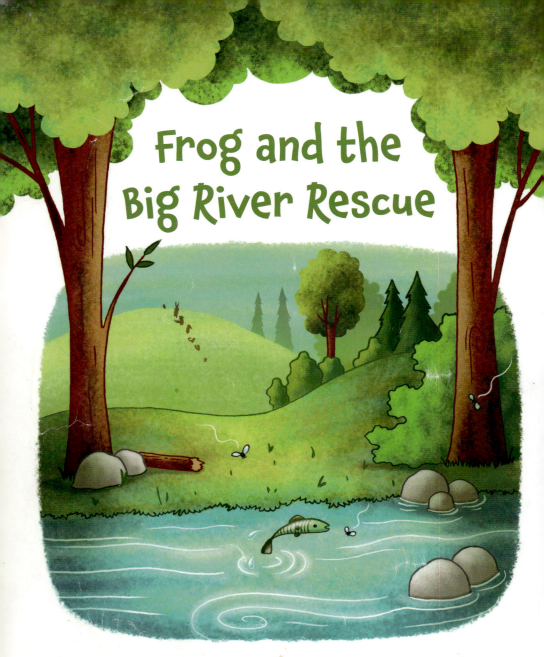

Frog and the Big River Rescue

Frog and his friends liked to picnic at

Big River.

There was good green grass and lots of acorns. Sometimes there were small sweet strawberries and always juicy, fruity bugs.

It was a sunny afternoon.

"Picnic time!" Frog said.

Frog, Squirrel, Chameleon, Possum with her babies, Raccoon, Rabbit, and little Jumping Mouse jumped, hopped, ran, and scampered down to Big River.

First they ate.

"Mmm, strawberries!" little Jumping Mouse said.

"Great bugs!" Chameleon said.

He and Frog had a game to see which

one of them had the longest tongue.

Chameleon won.

Rabbit and Possum talked about names for babies.

"I like One, Two, Three, Four, Five for mine," Possum said.

Rabbit said, "I just call all of mine 'Bunny.' I ran out of names a long time ago. I have had a lot of babies."

The little possums played hide-and-seek.

They ran races on the grass beside the river.

"Do not go too close to the water," Possum called to them.

Just then one little possum slipped and

fell in the river.

"Help! Help!" he screamed.

The fast water was carrying him away.

Possum leaped up. "I'm coming, Baby Five!" she called.

Frog held her back. "Do not go in the river," he cried. "You will not make it. I will go."

Frog jumped quickly into the river.

The water rushed around him.

It was not like swimming in his pond.

He swam his fastest toward little

Possum Five.

He kicked with his long back legs.

Faster, faster.

It was hard work. Would he be in time?

At last Frog reached the little one.

"Hold on to me," he called. "Get on my

back!"

Little Possum Five crawled onto Frog's

back.

"Hold tight!" Frog shouted.

Frog huffed and puffed. *Keep going*, he told himself. *Do not give up!*

Here was the riverbank. Thank
goodness!

Paws reached out to him. All kinds of
paws. They scooped little Possum Five off
his back.

They dragged them both on to the grass. Frog and little Possum Five had swallowed a lot of water.

Raccoon turned Frog on his stomach.

She pumped his back.

"Burp!" he burbled. "Burp!"

Water sloshed out.

Possum pressed on the little possum's back till he screamed, "Stop, Mama! You are hurting me."

"How can I thank you, Frog?" Possum

asked. "You were so brave. You are a true

hero."

His friends clapped. "You are! You are!"

"It was nothing," Frog told them.

"But it is bad to swim after you eat," Raccoon told Frog. "Remember that next time a little possum falls in."

"I will," Frog said.

Little Possum Five tugged at Frog's leg.

"That was fun," he said. "Can we do it again?"

"Fun?" Frog croaked. "Do it again?"

"My turn! My turn!" little

Possum Three shouted.

"Me! Me! Me!" They were all

tugging.

Frog sighed. "I need a nap!" he said.